This igloo book belongs to:

....

igloobooks

Published in 2019
by Igloo Books Ltd
Cottage Farm
Sywell
NN6 0BJ
www.igloobooks.com

GOL002 0219
6 8 10 11 9 7
ISBN 978-1-78557-916-5

Based on the original story by Rudyard Kipling
Illustrated by Jenny Wren
Written by Jenny Woods

Cover designed by Lee Italiano
Interiors designed by Justine Ablett
and Katie Messenger
Edited by Hannah Cather

Printed and manufactured in China

The Jungle Book

igloobooks

Deep in the jungle, a lost boy sat crying. The sound brought the fierce tiger, Shere Khan, **prowling** through the thick undergrowth. He had chased the boy's parents away and now he had come back for the child.

The tiger was just about to pounce when an enormous bear lumbered into the clearing. **"A man cub!"** gasped Baloo, the bear, in surprise. **"What's your name, child?"**

"Mowgli," said the boy, glancing up at the bear's kind, furry face. **"I know who will look after you,"** said Baloo and he called out to the wolf pack.

Shere Khan **growled** angrily. He had missed this chance to catch the boy, but there would be others.

Soon, Father Wolf and Mother Wolf appeared through the bushes.
"This is Mowgli," said Baloo, nudging the boy forward.

"Poor little cub," said Mother Wolf, giving Mowgli's face a gentle lick.
It tickled so much that he began to giggle.
"Don't worry, Baloo," said Father Wolf. **"We will take good care of him."**

Days later, Mowgli was playing happily with the wolf cubs. Suddenly, a furious **roar** thundered through the jungle and Shere Khan bounded out of the shadows. **"That's my man cub!"** he growled.

Mother Wolf leapt forward. **"Mowgli belongs to our pack now,"** she snapped. **"We will see,"** sneered the tiger, slinking away.

The next time the full moon glowed
in the night sky, Father Wolf took
Mowgli to the pack meeting.

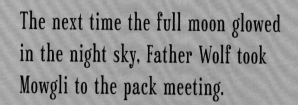

Akela, the leader of the wolves, looked down from his high rock
and asked, **"Why should we allow a man cub into our pack?"**
"Because Mowgli is my cub," answered Father Wolf, proudly.

Baloo held up a huge paw. **"I'll teach him the jungle laws,"** he promised. Then, Bagheera, the black panther, padded into the ring. **"And I'll watch over him,"** he purred. Akela nodded and all the wolves howled together.

Watching from his hiding place, Shere Khan **snarled** with rage.

So it was that Mowgli came to live among the wolves. Baloo taught him the ways of the jungle, and Mowgli would sit and listen to every **rustle** in the grass and every breath of the warm air.

But he would also hear the low **growl** of Shere Khan, as he **prowled** through the trees.

When Mowgli got bigger and stronger,
Father Wolf taught him how to run and hunt.

Soon, he was as **fast** as any of the pack.

But Mowgli loved his lessons with Baloo the best.
The bear showed him where to find juicy berries
and how to ask the bees for their sweet honey.

When Mowgli got too sticky,
he **splashed** in the jungle
pools and Baloo taught him
how to swim.

All the while,
Shere Khan watched...

... and waited.

As the years passed and Akela grew older and weaker, the tiger came to be great friends with the younger wolves. He asked them why they were happy to be led by an old wolf and a man cub.

Bagheera knew how dangerous Shere Khan was and warned Mowgli never to trust him. **"If you're ever in danger, fetch the red flower from the man village. All animals fear it,"** he said.

The red flower was actually fire, but the animals were too scared to say its name.

One day, when Mowgli was napping, the monkeys crept through the trees and **snatched** him away.

"Baloo!" cried Mowgli, fearfully. **"Help me!"**

Baloo and Bagheera heard his cries and rushed to Kaa, the snake, for help.

Meanwhile, the monkeys chattered noisily and carried Mowgli off to the ruins of the lost city. **"Man used to live here,"** said the monkeys. **"Now, it is ours."**

Kaa was the only creature that the monkeys feared.
As Baloo and Bagheera entered the lost city, the monkeys
pounced on them. Suddenly, Kaa slithered out from
the bushes, lifted his head and gave a loud hiSSS!

Shrieking with fear,
the monkeys ran away.

"Thank you for saving me," said Mowgli, hugging his friends.

On the other side of the jungle, Shere Khan was plotting a way to get hold of the man cub. The cunning tiger had persuaded the young wolves that Mowgli did not belong with them.

"Akela is getting older and weaker," he said. "It is Mowgli who will be leader of the pack when he dies."

"But if you choose your own leader, you can give Mowgli to me," purred Shere Khan.

"It's true. The boy doesn't belong in the pack," said the young wolves. "He is not one of us."

Father Wolf was hunting nearby. He had heard everything and ran off to warn Mowgli.

Mowgli would not believe Father Wolf. **"Akela is still strong enough to lead the pack,"** he said.

So, Father Wolf took him to watch the hunt. They peered through the leaves as the young wolves called out to their leader, **"Why don't you catch that fine stag, Akela?"**

The old wolf gathered all his strength and **leapt** at the stag. It jumped out of the way and gave Akela a sharp kick. The other wolves **howled** with laughter, but Mowgli felt sad. **"Akela can no longer protect me,"** he sighed. **"I know what I must do."**

Mowgli **dashed** through the jungle until he reached the man village. He crept up to one of the huts and peered through the window. Inside, a family were sitting around a fire, where lumps of charcoal glowed. When the family went to bed, Mowgli tiptoed inside, scooped up some glowing coals into a pot and left silently.

As Mowgli left the village, a howl **pierced** through the jungle. **"It is time for the pack meeting,"** he thought. When he arrived, Mowgli was horrified to see Shere Khan sitting on the high rock, while Akela was slumped on the ground.

"Your leader is doomed to die!" roared Shere Khan.

Mowgli sprang to his feet. **"What has a tiger to do with our leadership?"**

There were yells of, **"Silence, man cub! Let him speak."**

"Give me the man cub," snarled the tiger, "He is a man's child and from the marrow of my bones, I hate him!"

The wolves yelled, "A man! A man! What has a man to do with us? Let him go to his own place."

The young wolves gathered around, **growling** fiercely. Suddenly, Mowgli **jumped** onto the rocks, lifted the pot and threw its contents. The hot coals tumbled out, setting fire to the dry grass. Flames flared up around Shere Khan and he fled into the jungle, **yowling** in terror.

As Mowgli walked away from the fire, he knew it was time for him to leave his jungle home. **"It is not safe for me here any more,"** he said, sadly. **"You will be happy in the man village,"** said Mother Wolf, smiling.

"Goodbye, my friends. Thank you for taking care of me," said Mowgli. He set off towards the man village, knowing he'd never forget his friends.